create your own ...
PIZZERIA

Marta Dansa
text by Gina Samba

First American Edition 2016
Kane Miller, A Division of EDC Publishing

Copyright © Edicions Somnins 2010 S.L.
Illustrations copyright © Marta Dansa
Text copyright © Gina Samba

First published by Edicions Somnins 2010

somnins

For information contact:
Kane Miller, A Division of EDC Publishing
PO Box 470663
Tulsa, OK 74147-0663
www.kanemiller.com
www.edcpub.com
www.usbornebooksandmore.com

Library of Congress Control Number: 2015954189

Manufactured by Regent Publishing Services, Hong Kong
Printed June 2016 in ShenZhen, Guangdong, China

2 3 4 5 6 7 8 9 10

ISBN: 978-1-61067-439-3

Hi! I'm **Martina.**＊

And I'm **PABLO.**＊

create your own ...
PIZZERIA

With this book, you'll plan and design your very own pizza restaurant!

You get to pick a name, decide on the decor, figure out what equipment you need and create the most delicious pizzas ever.

When you're done, make up the menu, and get ready for your customers!

＊Martina and Pablo are here to help.

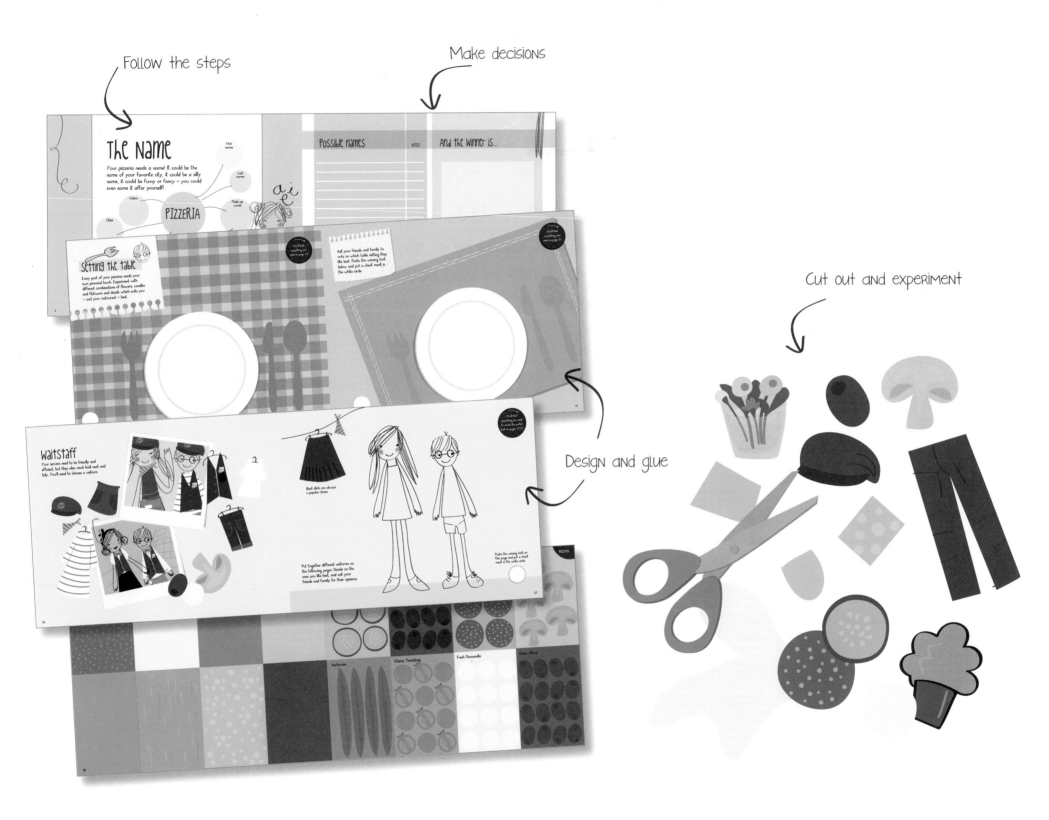

Follow the steps

Make decisions

Cut out and experiment

Design and glue

The Name

Your pizzeria needs a name! It could be the name of your favorite city, it could be a silly name, it could be funny or fancy – you could even name it after yourself!

PIZZERIA

Possible names

VOTES

And the winner is...

Setting the table

Every part of your pizzeria needs your own personal touch. Experiment with different combinations of flowers, candles and flatware and decide which suits you – and your restaurant – best.

Ask your friends and family to vote on which table setting they like best. Paste the winning look below and put a check mark in the white circle.

Waitstaff

Your servers need to be friendly and efficient, but they also must look neat and tidy. You'll need to choose a uniform.

Black shirts are always a popular choice

Put together different uniforms on the following pages. Decide on the ones you like best, and ask your friends and family for their opinions.

Anchovies

Cherry Tomatoes

Fresh Mozzarella

Green Olives

THE NAME

Your pizzeria needs a name! It could be the name of your favorite city, it could be a silly name, it could be funny or fancy — you could even name it after yourself!

First names

Last names

Colors

Made-up words

PIZZERIA

Cities

Foods

Pretty words

Pizza Roma

THE GOLDEN TOMATO

PRETTY PIES

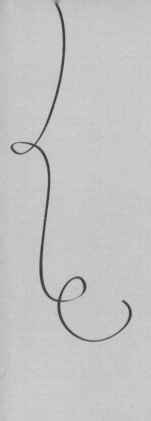

Possible names

VOTES

And the winner is...

Ask your friends and family to vote for the name they like the best.

The Logo

Designing a logo for your restaurant is an important step. Using your logo on menus, signs, uniforms and elsewhere helps identify your business and show everyone what it's all about.

Pick a background, add the name of your restaurant and then choose an image (or two)!

You'll find everything you need on page 33.

Images to add

There are so many possibilities!

Write the name of your pizzeria.

MAX's
Good Pizza

Fonts to create your logo

The Best
Pizzeria

Roma
Good Pizza

6

Lettering Style

The name of your pizzeria is the most important part of your logo. Try out different lettering styles – does plain, fancy, decorated or simple make it look best?

Practice different styles and designs on a piece of paper, then paste the one you like best below.

Location! Location! Location!

Choosing the right location for a restaurant isn't easy, but don't worry! The perfect spot could be just around the corner ...

FiX it UP!

A fresh coat of paint, a new awning and a plant or two will make your space look brand new.

Idea!
Planters or fresh flowers near the front door will make your restaurant look even more inviting!

After ...

Before ...

You'll find everything you need to fix things up on page 35.

The Pizza!

The pizza crust is as important as what goes on top of it! Thick or thin, it's up to you, just make sure you love the way it tastes (and that other people do too). Practice makes perfect! A basic recipe follows ...

INGREDIENTS
3 ¾ cups all-purpose flour
1 tbsp olive oil
1 tbsp fast-acting yeast
1 tsp salt
1 cup lukewarm water
½ tsp sugar

Basic Pizza Dough

Put the flour, the yeast, the salt and the sugar in a big mixing bowl. Stir until everything is combined, then add the olive oil and the water. Mix everything together, then turn the dough out onto a floured board and knead for 3-5 minutes.

Form the dough back into a ball and place it in a clean, oiled bowl. Cover with a dish towel and let rise in a warm place until double in size.

Punch the dough down, then divide it into two equal pieces. Shape the pieces into round balls and let them rest for 4-6 minutes. Roll each ball out on a floured surface into a 12" circle (or a 16" circle – a wider circle means a thinner crust).

Place the dough on a lightly oiled pizza pan or sheet, and let it rise for 10-15 minutes. Now it's time to add your toppings! Sauce, cheese, whatever you like, now's the time. Place the pan on the bottom rack of a cold oven, turn the oven to 500 degrees (get an adult to help) and bake 17-20 minutes until done.

Take a photo of your creation, then dig in!

Tip!

The dough has been kneaded enough when it no longer sticks to your hands. If you've been kneading for a while and it still sticks, add a little more flour.

The Pizza!

You want your pizzeria to be memorable, and you want a reason for people to keep coming back to your restaurant! Customers sometimes like to try new things. On these pages you can experiment with both common toppings and new combinations. Discuss your ideas with your friends and family and decide on your restaurant's specialties! And don't forget to give them interesting names!

You'll find ingredients to cut out and paste here on pages 37-39.

Classic Pizzas

Margarita
Tomato, mozzarella and fresh basil

Pepperoni
Tomato, mozzarella and pepperoni

Mushroom
Tomato, mozzarella and mushrooms

Hawaiian
Tomato, mozzarella, ham, and pineapple

Pizza:

Pizza:

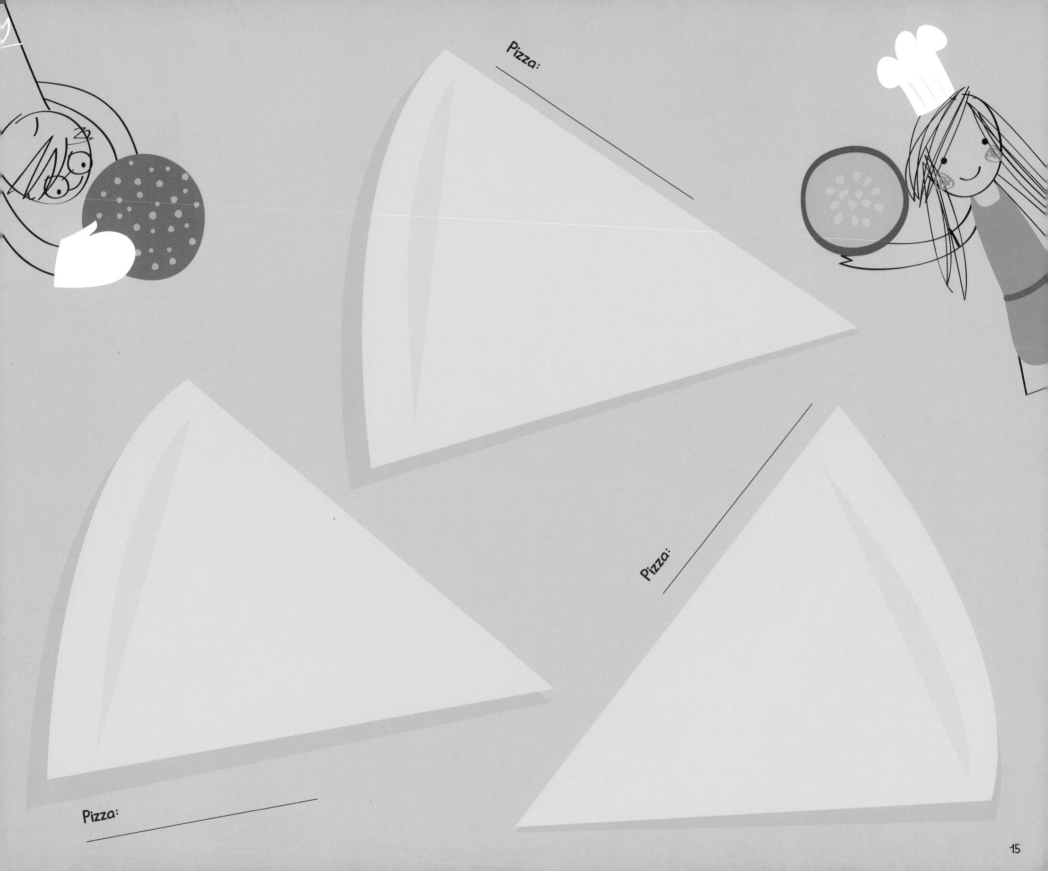

Pizza: _____

Pizza: _____

Pizza: _____

Pizza: _____

Challenge yourself!
What's the very best pizza
you can imagine?

You'll find ingredients to cut out and paste here on pages 37-39.

GO CRAZY!

What about a pizza that looks like a fac

Setting the table

Every part of your pizzeria needs your own personal touch. Experiment with different combinations of flowers, candles and flatware and decide which suits you — and your restaurant — best.

You'll find everything you need on page 41.

Ask your friends and family to vote on which table setting they like best. Paste the winning look below and put a check mark in the white circle.

You'll find everything you need on page 41.

Napkin folding

Practice folding these shapes with a cloth or paper napkin. Your customers will love them.

Remember that napkins can be placed on top of the plate, next to the fork or even inside a glass or cup.

Try these shapes:

Fan

1
Pleat the entire napkin by folding it back and forth.

2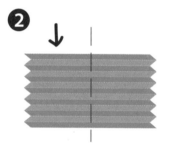
Press the pleats tightly together and mark the center.

3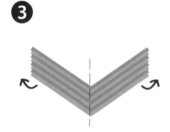
Fold the napkin in half.

4
Place it inside a glass or cup and let it fall open.

Candle

1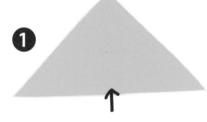
With the napkin open on the table, fold it in half into a triangle.

2
Make another small fold toward the top.

3
Turn the napkin over. Take one end and roll it as you see in the drawing.

4
Tuck the final end into the folded hem.

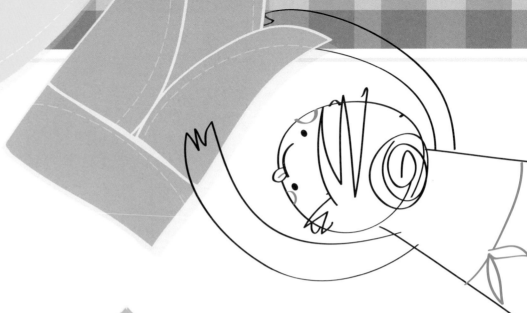

Lotus flower

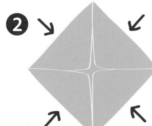 **1** With the napkin open on the table, fold each corner in toward the center as shown.

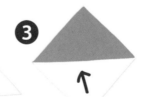 **2** Fold the corners in to the center again.

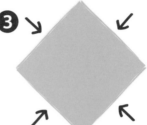 **3** Flip the napkin over on the table.

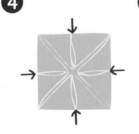 **4** Fold the corners in to the center.

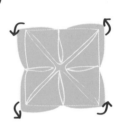 **5** Lift and unfold the corners underneath.

Lily

1 With the napkin open on the table, fold into a triangle.

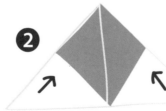 **2** Fold the two corners in to meet at the top point.

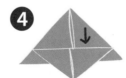 **3** Fold in half from the bottom up, making a triangle.

4 Unfold partway down as shown.

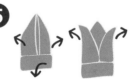 **5** Hide the bottom at the back. Turn the sides to the back and attach them one to the other.

You can't do it all

A pizzeria needs waitstaff and cooks. Depending on the size of your restaurant, you might also need a dishwasher, busboys and a manager. Let's get started!

Your Staff

Attach photos or draw pictures of the people who'll make up your staff. They could be friends, relatives, or even people you haven't met yet! What a great team!

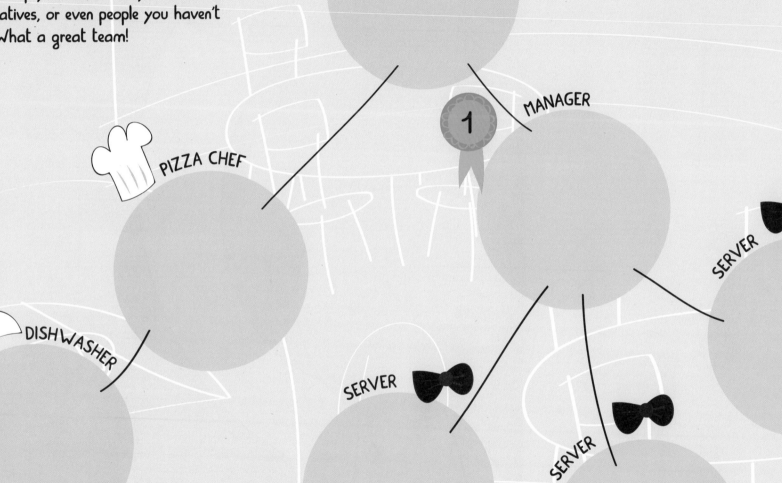

OWNER

MANAGER

PIZZA CHEF

SERVER

DISHWASHER

SERVER

SERVER

1

23

The pizza chef!

You can't have a pizzeria without this very important person. Who will yours be? What will they look like?

You'll find everything you need for your chef on page 43.

The Manager

The manager is in charge of the staff. Who will yours be? What will they look like?

You'll find everything you need for your manager on page 45.

25

Waitstaff

Your servers need to be friendly and efficient, but they also must look neat and tidy. You'll need to choose a uniform.

Black skirts are always a popular choice.

You'll find everything you need to create the perfect look on pages 47-51.

Put together different uniforms on the following pages. Decide on the ones you like best, and ask your friends and family for their opinions.

Paste the winning look on this page and put a check mark in the white circle.

Sporty or classic?

What about a hat?
It's a good idea to
keep hair covered.

You'll find everything you need to create the perfect look on pages 47-51.

What does it cost?

Now that you know what your restaurant will look like, what kinds of pizzas you'll serve, and who will make up your staff, you need to figure out how much to charge for your food. Let's add it up ...

Let's have a look:

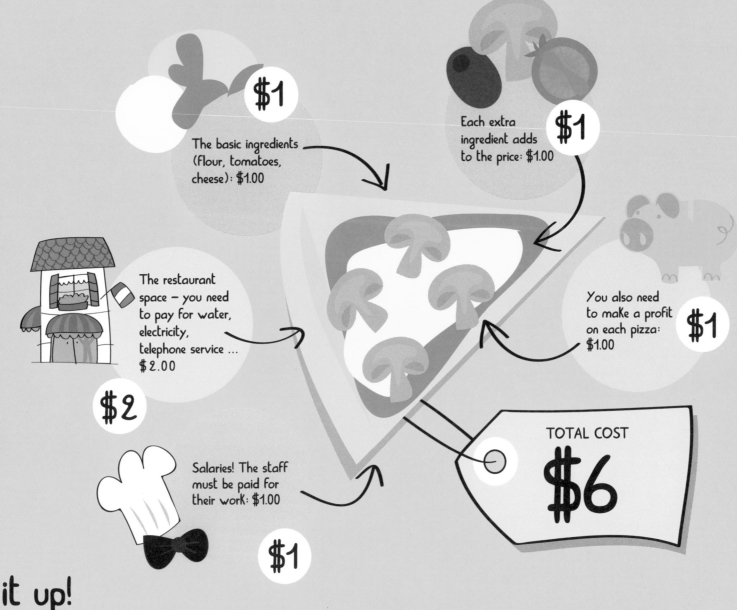

$1

The basic ingredients (flour, tomatoes, cheese): $1.00

$1

Each extra ingredient adds to the price: $1.00

$2

The restaurant space — you need to pay for water, electricity, telephone service ... $2.00

$1

You also need to make a profit on each pizza: $1.00

$1

Salaries! The staff must be paid for their work: $1.00

TOTAL COST
$6

Add it up!

Now you know how much goes into a mushroom pizza. Try it with one of your specialty pizzas too.

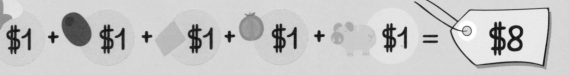

$2 + $1 + $1 + $1 + $1 + $1 + $1 = $8

Patterns, papers and designs

Use the small pictures for your logo.

Good Pizza

Pizzeria

Save the larger ones for your menu.

Good Pizza

Pizzeria

Does your restaurant need a new roof?

Plants and flowers make a space more inviting.

Something fun?

Umbrellas make outdoor dining more comfortable.

More decorations!

Pretty awnings add shade – and charm!

What about a fence along the patio?

m

Tomato Sauce

Cheese

Salami

en Peppers

Sausage

Tuna Fish

Tomato Sauce

37

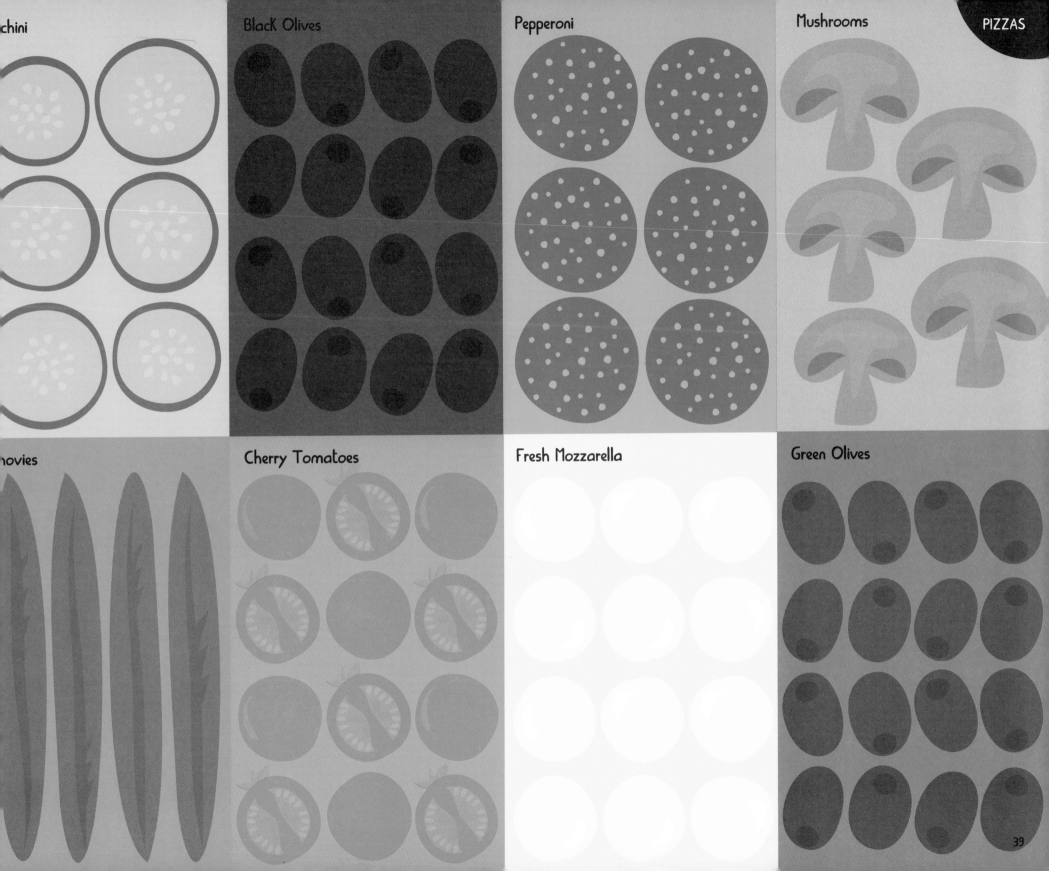

chini

Black Olives

Pepperoni

Mushrooms

PIZZAS

novies

Cherry Tomatoes

Fresh Mozzarella

Green Olives

39

Traditional

Artisan

Practical

Modern

Professional

Serious

Silly

Friendly

Beginner

n°1

★★★
★★

FAST

Expert

Classic

Traditional

Daring

Serious

Name:

Name:

Elegant

Flirty

Chic

Funny

45

Try out different uniform combinations. It's fun!

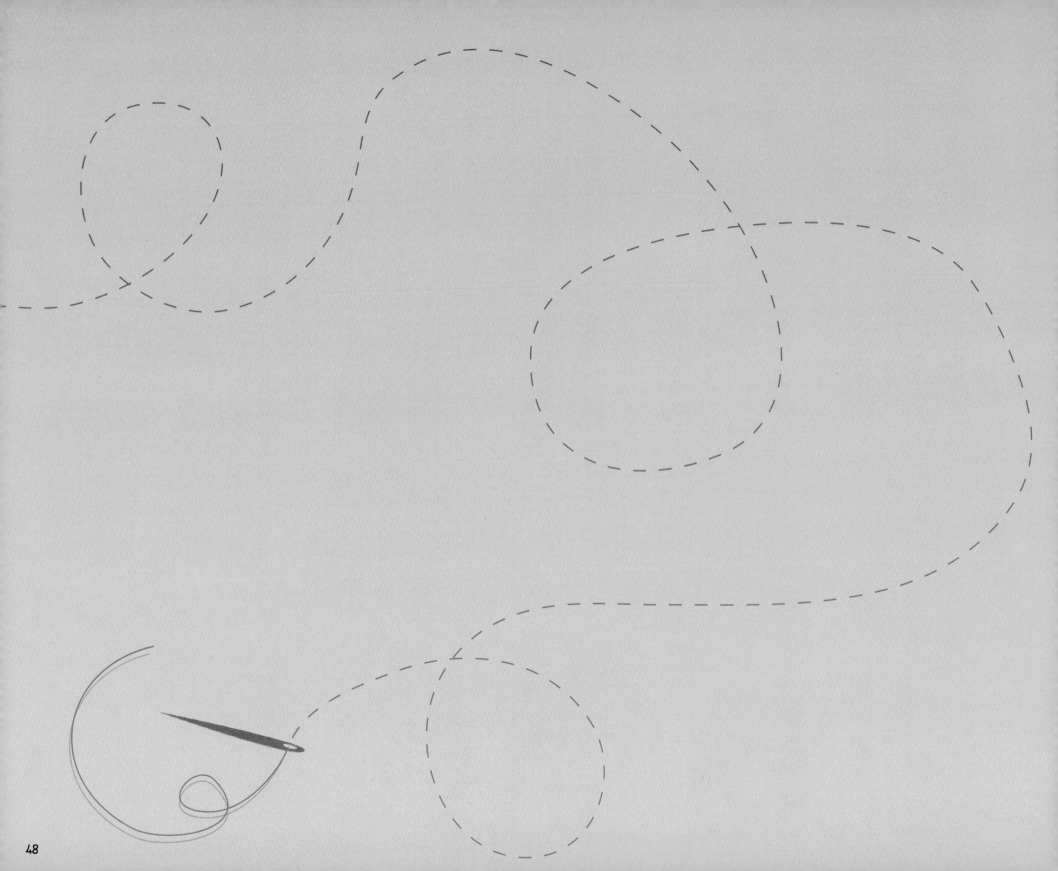

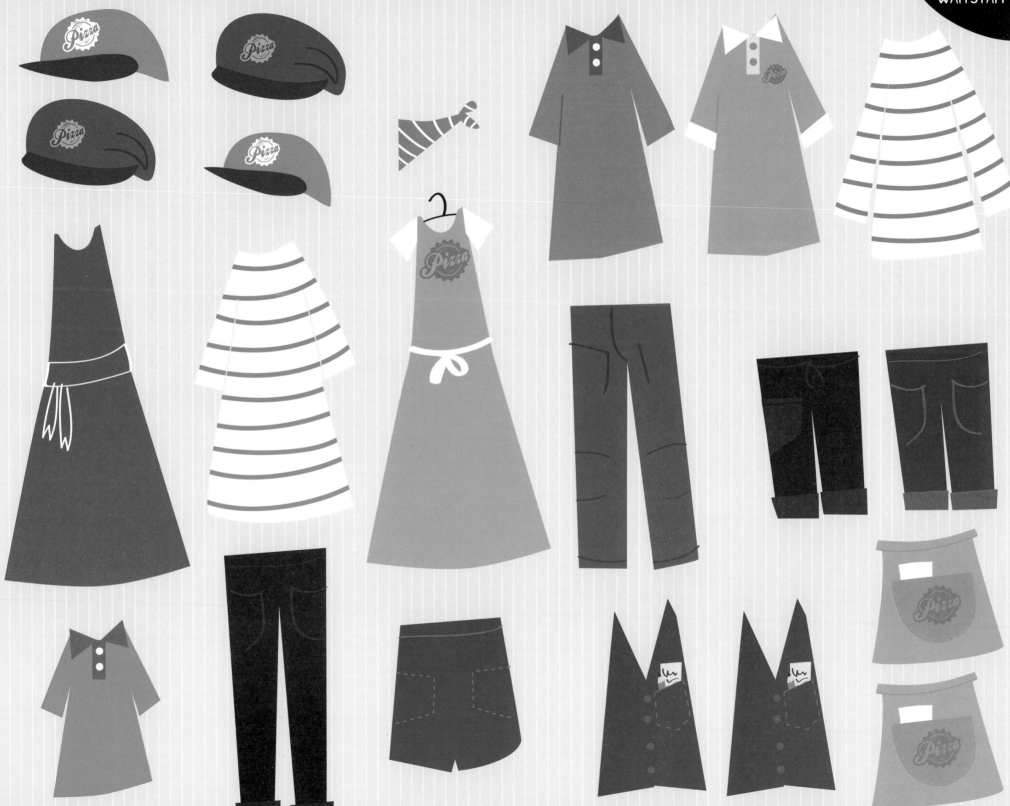

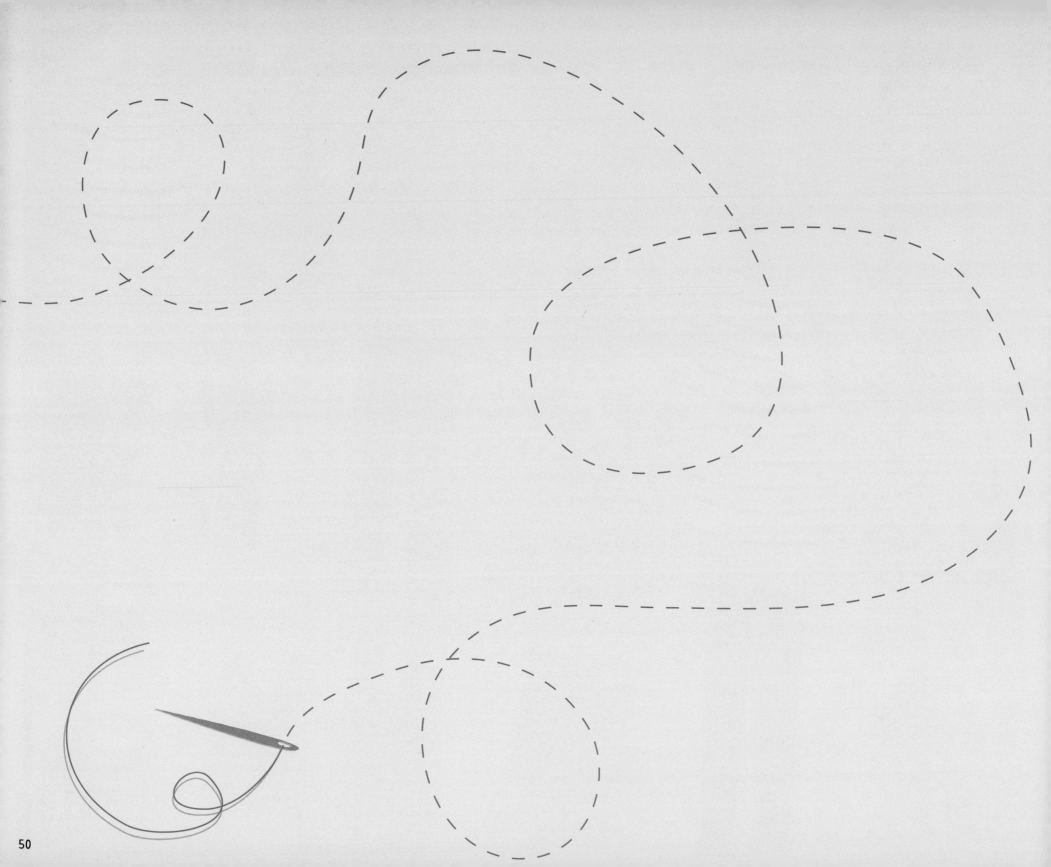

Designing the menu

Now that you've figured out exactly what your pizza restaurant will be like, design your best menu and share it with your friends. It's so much fun to have a restaurant!

The menu

Choose and paste ...

You'll find everything you need to create your menu on the following pages.

Your favorite desserts

The children's menu

The perfect patio

The address and telephone number of your pizzeria. Draw a map too, so customers can find you.

MENU

Your logo

The appetizers and small plates you'll offer

Pizzas of the day

The pizzas

The drinks you'll serve

Appetizers and Drinks

Spaghetti with pesto

Minestrone soup

Ravioli with tomato sauce

Potato soup

Green salad

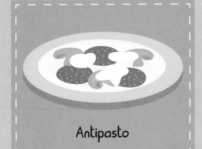

Antipasto

Caesar salad

Lasagna

Espresso

Cappuccino

Latte

Hot chocolate

Red wine

Rosé

White wine

Sparkling wine

Cola

Ginger ale

Beer

Sparkling water

Apple juice

Orange juice

Lemonade

Water

Pineapple juice

Tomato juice

Grape juice

Hot tea

55

Desserts

Which desserts will your restaurant serve? Make up interesting names and paste the desserts on the following page.

Children's Menu

Decide on two children's meals for your menu.

GAMES FOR THE MENU

It's a good idea to print a game on the menu – that way, children have something to do while they wait for their meal. Which game do you like best?

Look at the first fruit cup. Can you spot what's missing in the other three?

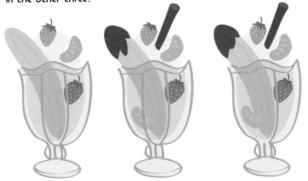

Follow the spaghetti trails. Where does each end up?

1 → ⬤
2 → ⬤
3 → ⬤
4 → ⬤

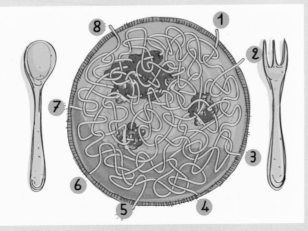

CHILDREN'S MENU

RED MENU

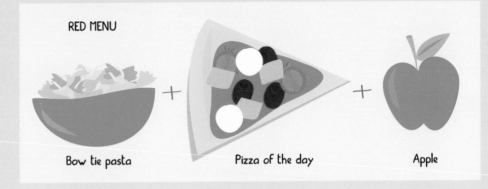

Bow tie pasta + Pizza of the day + Apple

PURPLE MENU

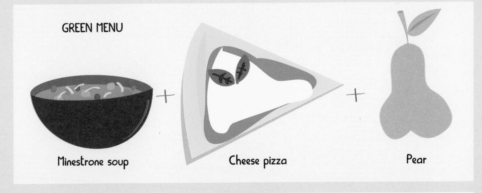

Spaghetti with pesto + Pepperoni pizza + Ice cream cone

GREEN MENU

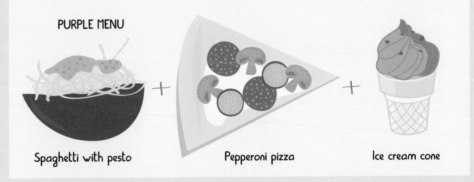

Minestrone soup + Cheese pizza + Pear

ORANGE MENU

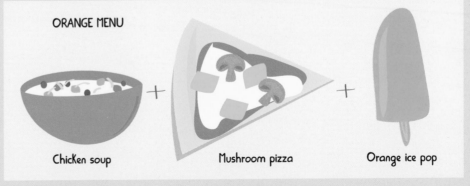

Chicken soup + Mushroom pizza + Orange ice pop

The Patio

You've got six different patios to choose from. Which suits your pizzeria best? Cut out the one you like best and paste it on your menu page.

Remember to look at all the choices, here and on the next page, before you decide!